P9-DBO-193

Ada Lace, on the Case

For the quiet girls who have the loudest minds
and the boldest dreams
—E. C.

For Milo
—T. W.

For Zoey. I hope you'll always be just as curious as Ada.
—R. K.

SIMON & SCHUSTER BOOKS FOR YOUNG READERS
An imprint of Simon & Schuster Children's Publishing Division
1230 Avenue of the Americas, New York, New York 10020
This book is a work of fiction. Any references to historical events, real people, or real places are used fictitiously. Other names, characters, places, and events are products of the author's imagination, and any resemblance to actual events or places or persons, living or dead, is entirely coincidental.

Also available in a Simon & Schuster Books for Young Readers paperback edition
Book design by Laurent Linn
The text for this book was set in Minister Std.
The illustrations for this book were rendered in Adobe Photoshop.
Manufactured in the United States of America
0220 FFG
First Simon & Schuster Books for Young Readers hardcover edition August 2017
4 6 8 10 9 7 5 3
Library of Congress Cataloging-in-Publication Data
Names: Calandrelli, Emily, author. | Kurilla, Renée, illustrator.
Title: Ada Lace, on the case : an Ada Lace adventure / Emily Calandrelli ;
illustrated by Renée Kurilla.
Description: First edition. | New York :
Simon & Schuster Books for Young Readers, [2017]
Identifiers: LCCN 2016037012 | ISBN 9781481485999 (hardcover : alk. paper) |
ISBN 9781481485982 (pbk. : alk. paper) | ISBN 9781481486002 (eBook)
Subjects: | CYAC: Mystery and detective stories. | Science—Methodology—Fiction.
Classification: LCC PZ7.1.C28 Ad 2017 | DDC [Fic]—dc23
LC record available at https://lccn.loc.gov/2016037012

Ada Lace, on the Case

· AN ADA LACE ADVENTURE ·

EMILY CALANDRELLI

WITH TAMSON WESTON

ILLUSTRATED BY RENÉE KURILLA

Simon & Schuster Books for Young Readers

New York London Toronto Sydney New Delhi

Chapter One

Good-Bye with a Side of Bacon

Ada was sick of sitting. She was sick of the cast on her leg. She was sick of watching the world go by without her. She should be outside, exploring the neighborhood and researching the local wildlife, but she was stuck inside. And it was her own fault.

Their first week in San Francisco, Ada had attempted a bungee jump from a eucalyptus tree in the park. It was a jump she could have made with no bungee. The bungee was capable of stretching 50 percent of its length with her attached to it, but the branch was barely high enough to make the line taut. It was a careless mistake.

While Ada was brooding, her mom came in.

"Do you think you might come have breakfast with me before I go?" her mother asked.

"I guess so. I was hoping we could skip the good-bye part," said Ada.

"I'll only be gone for a few days," said Ada's mom. "These artists need a little bit of hand-holding. They aren't as tough as you are. I'll be back in time for your first day at school."

Ada attempted a smile and, on her crutches, followed her mom down the stairs only to be nearly flattened by her brother, Elliott, outside the kitchen. He was wearing an eyepatch and a vest. A stuffed parrot hung lamely from his shoulder. Ada had been reading *Treasure Island* with Elliott. Now Elliott was determined to find buried treasure. Until then he was dressing the part.

"Easy there, mate," said Ada's mom. "You almost capsized your sister."

"Yarr!" said Elliott. "That's 'Captain' to you. Get that straight, lady, or you'll walk the plank!"

"Tone it down, Elliott, or you'll spend the weekend in your room," said Ms. Lace.

"Sorry, me lady," said Elliott.

"Do I have to make you swab the poop deck, Elliott?" asked Mr. Lace. He placed a plate of French toast in front of Ada. It had crossed eyes.

"Thanks, Pop," said Ada. It was hard to stay grumpy around her dad.

"This blasted parrot won't sit!" said Elliott.

"You need to secure his tail feathers." Ada wrapped the string around the parrot's tail and feet then tied it. "That requires a square knot. What you had was a granny."

"Arrgh! There ye be, Ruffles. Good bird," said Elliott.

"Ada, do you remember that lady we met at the farmer's market? Glenda?" asked Ada's mom. "Her daughter's about your age. They live over on Polymer Street. You should get together with her."

"And do what, jump rope?" said Ada, looking down at her cast.

"Very funny," said Ada's mom. "How about you have her over?"

Ada shrugged. She wasn't in the mood to entertain.

"It would give you a head start on being the new kid," said Ada's mom. She stood, stuffing one last piece of bacon in her mouth. "Just think about it. I'll leave the phone number."

"Kay," said Ada. Her mom gave her a kiss on the cheek. Ms. Lace hugged her husband and her son and collected her bags.

"Bon voyage!" yelled Elliott. "Bring me back some gold!"

Ada's mom squatted beside Ada's chair. "Cheer up, sweet pea. You'll be the queen of Juniper Garden before you know it."

Chapter Two

Juniper Garden

After her mom left, Ada returned to her room to unpack the last few boxes. As she opened the first one, she was lost in a sea of memories. In it were soil samples, rocks, and some pressed leaves from the woods by her old house in West Virginia. The whole box smelled like West Virginia. There was also last year's science project, which she'd worked on with her friend Anna. Anna and Ada had been partners in everything. They'd had a pet-sitting business together, and they had been three-legged race partners on field day. They had even placed first and second in the spelling bee. Most important, they had always been science project partners. Everyone called them A&A, but they called themselves A^2.

Ada gazed out her window at her new neighborhood. The back of her family's town house faced a common area shared by a circle of small apartment buildings and other town houses. There was a fountain in the center of the courtyard. Elliott was in the middle of a fierce foam sword fight with his new friend Jack, a kid who lived on Polymer. To her left, Jacob Swift was on his patio filling his bird feeders and hanging a big blob of fatty suet for the woodpeckers. Jacob was one of the first neighbors Ada and her family had met. He was dressed for work. *He probably works for some cool tech company,* she thought.

Next to Jacob's building was a brick building. Ada had seen an older man with orangey-brown coveralls walking out of it the other day, but she hadn't met him yet. To the right of his building was an alleyway that led to a street on the other side of Juniper Garden. To the right of the alley were five more buildings that curved around the courtyard, and another small driveway with metal gates. Ada looked over at Jacob's patio again. A bunch of birds had gathered around the feeder. There were finches of different colors and a lot of sparrows. She saw Jacob standing at his back door, smiling. From the apartment two floors above him, Jeanie Frances watched too.

A squirrel came and muscled out the birds. Then a little Yorkshire terrier ran from the ground floor apartment at the far right side of Juniper Garden. The dog barked and barked and scared every living thing away. The terrier's owner, Ms. Reed, came out of her apartment chattering on her phone. She talked so loudly, Ada could make out every word.

"I *know*," Ms. Reed said. "They have no business putting something that expensive on the registry. . . ."

The man in coveralls came out the back door of the building next to Jacob's. Mr. Coveralls bent down and whistled, holding his hand out toward Ms. Reed's dog, which trotted over to him.

"MARGUERITE!" Ms. Reed yelled. The dog romped happily back to her owner. Ms. Reed let her inside. The man in the coveralls looked disappointed.

Jacob came back outside with a leather case and a newspaper. He handed Mr. Coveralls his paper with a friendly nod, then walked down the alley that led to Polymer Street. Mr. Coveralls headed back inside. A few minutes later Jeanie came down dressed in wide-legged trousers and carrying a blue case. She looked like she could work at the gallery where Ada's mom was the curator.

Ada instantly felt lonely thinking about her mom. Ms. Lace was away meeting a new artist, which wasn't unusual. But did she have to go so soon after the move? It was hard enough being in a new place with Mom at home and with a healthy leg.

Ada hobbled over to the bookshelf and pulled out a book about Charles Darwin's Galapagos journey. It had a bunch of his field notes in it. She sat back by the window and tried to read but couldn't focus because her foot itched. She grabbed a pencil and tried to scratch it, but the pencil wasn't long enough. She picked up a ruler from her desk, but the ruler was too thick to fit inside the cast. The itch grew and spread! It danced up and down her leg. Ada searched desperately around her room for the right tool.

On the shelf above her desk, Hydrogen and Oxygen, her two pet turtles, were having a slow tug-of-war with a carrot. Next to their tank she spotted an old radio antenna that she had rescued from the trash. She hoisted herself up on a crutch and reached up for the shelf. Her fingertips just touched the antenna, but it rolled away from her and down behind the desk. The itch itched more. It tickled. It burned! She knew it was really just a feedback loop in her neurons, but that didn't make it less annoying.

"AAAAARRRRRGGGGHHH!" Ada collapsed into her chair and scratched at her cast.

"Ada? Are you okay?" called her father.

"I'm dying of an itch!" said Ada. She could hear him rattling around in the kitchen. A minute later he appeared at her bedroom door.

Ada examined the pen, the spoon, and chopstick her dad offered her. She chose the chopstick, slid it under her cast, and scratched, scratched, scratched. It was beautiful.

"Thanks, Pop."

Relieved, she grabbed a field guide. Ada had started keeping field guides after reading about Charles Darwin on the *Beagle*. Her mother had encouraged her to keep a diary before the move, but Ada couldn't get into it. The field guides were a better fit. She liked the idea of keeping track of what was going on around her and kept her entries to the facts. She liked facts.

10:00–10:45 a.m. Read 15 more pages in the Darwin book. Still haven't gotten to the Galapagos.

10:45–10:46 a.m. Timed how long it took for an ant to crawl across the windowsill. (24 seconds to cover 60 cm).

11–11:05 a.m. Hung my head off the side of the bed. Results unclear, but slightly dizzy.

12:00–12:30 p.m. Ate Pop's famous tuna fish sandwich. The pickles were extra crisp this time.

1:00 p.m. Fed Hydrogen and Oxygen 4 pieces of cucumber and 2 strawberries. H&O_2 are good at eating—so slow and careful. I wonder if turtles can get fat?

She read her notes, which made it very clear how boring her day was. Now her boredom was preserved for future generations.

Chapter Three

ALOHA

At 1:57 Ada heard a "YARRRR!"

1:57 p.m. Elliott's home

"Batten down the hatches! Hoist the main! Shiver me timbers!" Elliott shouted. He ran up the stairs and stopped in front of Ada's room.

"Welcome home, Captain," said Ada.

"So long, m'lady. I'm off to fight the Royal Navy!"

Just like that Elliott was gone again. Ada supposed it was time to finish unpacking.

Then Ada's dad's head popped in the door. "You have company! Glenda's daughter . . ." The visitor burst in from behind him.

"Aloha! I'm Nina," Ada's unfamiliar guest sang. She had two buns on either side of her head and was dressed in every color imaginable.

"Do you know that 'aloha' doesn't just mean 'hello'? It's the combination of 'presence' and 'life,' and can be used as a good-bye or a form of welcome. Pretty cool, huh?"

Ada had never heard anyone sound so excited.

Nina floated around Ada's room, examining things. "Examining" wasn't the right word. She was . . . dancing with them, ogling them, maybe even casting a few spells on them. She picked up

ADA'S
ADA'S ROOM
SLIDES

Ada's test tube rack from her first chemistry set. She tried on Ada's night vision goggles. She took a peek in the box that Ada had half unpacked. She put on Ada's homemade gecko gloves and gazed at her hands. She held up every slide under Ada's microscope and found a different adjective for each.

"Flamboyant! Rotund! Scintillating! Tubular!"

Ada was impressed with Nina's vocabulary, though she kind of wished Nina would stop touching all of her stuff.

"Your room has such great energy," said Nina.

"Well, thanks," Ada said as she straightened the equipment left awry in Nina's wake.

"Turtles! Oh my goodness! They are soooo cute!" said Nina. She was

just about to reach in Hydrogen and Oxygen's tank when the high whine of a small engine caught her attention.

"Uh-oh. I bet that's Milton Edison." She ran to the window.

Ada propped herself up on a crutch to have a look. Outside in the garden, Milton, a boy who lived three buildings to the right of the alley in a fancy town house, watched a drone floating around the courtyard. All attention seemed to turn to the drone. Jack and Elliott dropped their swords, Mr. Coveralls came to the window, and Ms. Reed's little dog barked viciously. Milton zoomed the aircraft just above Marguerite. Her fur was stirred by

the air from the rotors. Marguerite yelped and ran back to her door. Ms. Reed came outside.

"Milton Edison, you keep that thing away from my Marguerite!"

"I was just flying it, Ms. R. Marguerite was the one who wanted a closer look."

"I wonder if you have the proper registration for such an aircraft."

Milton landed the drone, picked it up, and ran out of the garden by way of the alley.

"Wow. You have the best view ever!" Nina said. "It's like *Popperly Way*, only in real life!"

"What's *Popperly Way*?"

"It's a show I watch with my aunt. It's all about a neighborhood and how people get along—or don't get along. Like a . . . a . . . you know, like in a pond with frogs and flies and lily pads and algae and all that?"

"An ecosystem," said Ada.

"Yes! Exactly. An ecosystem. There's a whole cycle of energy to an ecosystem, you know?"

"I do," said Ada, gazing out the window at the scene below.

She watched as Mr. Coveralls read the newspaper that Jacob Swift had given him. Someone turned on a radio to a jazz station. Jack and Elliott threw a stick for Marguerite, while Ms. Reed watched from her patio, drinking a cup of tea. Ada smiled.

"I sure do," she said.

Chapter Four

THE URBAN ECOSYSTEM

Ada was excited to have something new to occupy her time: observing the Juniper Garden ecosystem.

Ada was so excited about observing the Juniper Garden ecosystem, she woke at 6:00 the next morning. She took her field guide and her favorite pencil to the window to record her findings.

6:03 a.m. Partly cloudy

4 humans, 3 squirrels, 6 finches, 22 sparrows, and a dog are present.

Observations:

Ms. Reed left her apartment with Marguerite at 6:15 a.m. She was not on the phone.

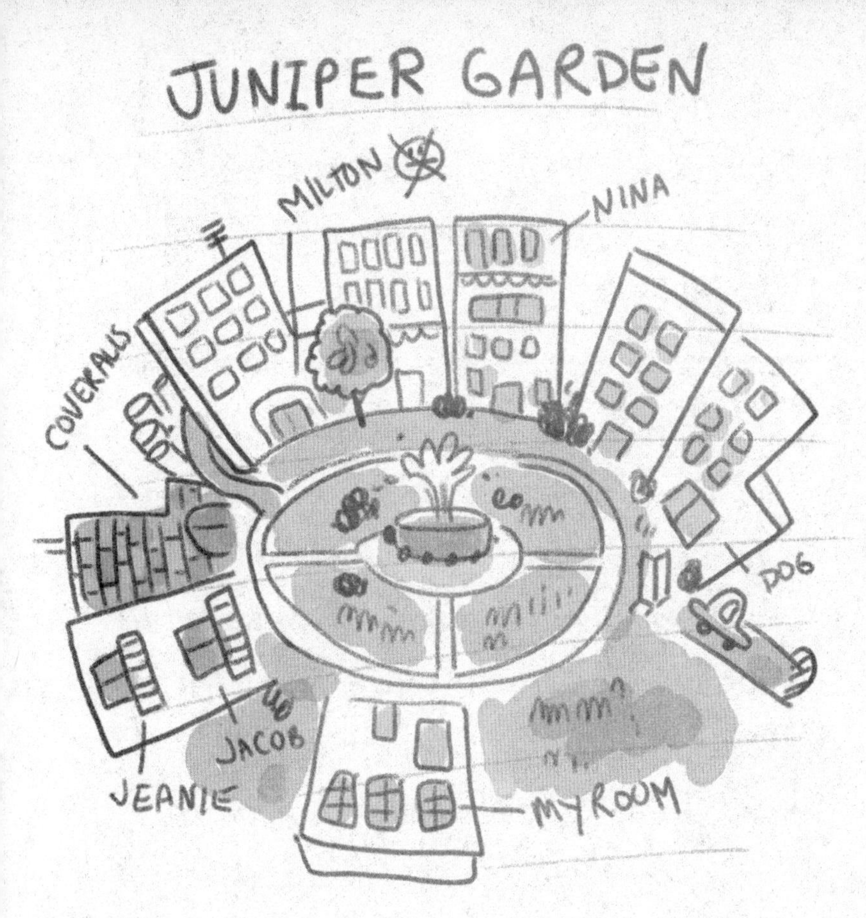

Jacob Swift hung an old record just above the bird feeder. I didn't know what it was for, but now I do! When a squirrel steps on the record to get to the feeder, the record starts to spin, and the squirrel goes flying. Clever invention . . .

Mr. Coveralls came downstairs with a cup of coffee. He watched the birds for a while and then went back upstairs.

Jacob came through the alley with Jeanie. They were dressed in running clothes.

7:00 a.m. Jacob dropped a bunch of wire and a newspaper by Mr. Coverall's building. Then he walked down the alley to the back street. Wonder what the wire is for?

Found out the shrubs by the fountain are Juniperus californica (Ah—that must be why this place is called Juniper Garden!).

7:25 a.m. Mr. Coveralls came downstairs and picked up the coil of wire and the paper and took them inside.

Ada left the window to have breakfast with her dad and brother. Then she finished unpacking before getting back to her field guide.

11:02 a.m. Returned to see Mr. Coveralls walking in with a bag from the thrift shop.

Elliott and Jack are playing with Marguerite again.

12:00 p.m. Pop's tuna fish is especially spicy today.

Mr. Coveralls has a fish tank with lots of colorful fish. Will need better binoculars to tell what kind they are.

Ada reached for her stronger binoculars.

"You wouldn't *believe* what happened today," Nina said.

Ada nearly jumped out of her skin. She was so focused on the garden that she hadn't noticed Nina come in.

"Oh. Hi, Nina. How'd you get in?"

"Your dad let me in. I told my sitter Rita to go home," said Nina. "You know, so we could hang out."

"Oh! Okay," said Ada. She looked out the window with her binoculars.

"Anyway, she's pretty shaken up. We had a pretty traumatic event today," said Nina. "Rita dropped my mom's mirror and broke it!"

"Did she cut herself?" asked Ada.

"No. But she dropped a *mirror*, Ada," said Nina. "*A mirror.* That's bad news."

"Did you get it all cleaned up?" asked Ada.

"That's not the point. Anyway, I gave her all my best amulets. My four-leaf clover, my favorite fortune-cookie fortune . . . Hopefully, that will do the trick," said Nina. "Maybe I can find a horseshoe in Golden Gate Park. . . ."

Ada looked at Nina blankly.

"Everyone knows breaking a mirror is seven years' bad luck!" said Nina.

"Right," Ada said. "But it should be okay, since there's no scientific evidence for luck."

"Oh well . . . maybe not yet," said Nina. "So what's happening on our version of *Popperly Way*?"

"Mr. Coveralls brought home a bag from the thrift shop," said Ada.

"Who's Mr. . . . OH! Mr. Peebles. Yeah, he's a weirdo. He's always collecting weird stuff," said Nina. "Broken vacuum cleaners, blenders, microwave ovens, old radios, satellite dishes . . ."

Ada could imagine creating some cool gadgets out of those items.

"I wonder what he does with it all," said Ada.

"What if he's building a spaceship?" said Nina.

"The probability of that seems low," Ada said.

Nina laughed. "But it's kind of fun to think about, right?"

"Huh. I guess it is," said Ada.

Another engine's whine came from below. It was not quite the same tone as the sound from the day before.

"Milton Edison," said Nina. Her expression darkened.

Sure enough, a big, knobby-tired truck came bumping around the fence by the side alley into the garden. Milton Edison stood at a distance with his remote. The truck raced toward Marguerite.

"RrrrrrRUCK! RUCK! RUCK! RUCK!" barked Marguerite.

"It sounds like she's saying 'truck'!" said Nina.

Ada giggled; it was kind of true. Marguerite chased after the truck. The truck made a U-turn and chased Marguerite back in the other direction. She seemed to be having fun. Ada and Nina laughed as they watched. But Ada guessed that Ms. Reed wouldn't find the show as funny as they did. She was right.

"Milton Edison! I'm telling your mother!"

yelled Ms. Reed from her back door. She pulled her phone out of her pocket to show that she meant business.

Milton's monster truck whizzed back toward Milton. Milton grabbed the truck and ran out of sight. Ms. Reed put her phone away. She called Marguerite, who trotted back to the door, wagging her tail. For the moment, the garden was peaceful.

Ada took out her field guide to jot down what she had just seen.

"Is that a diary?" asked Nina.

"It's a field guide for our ecosystem," said Ada. "This way I can keep track of what's happening in Juniper Garden."

"So, it's like a diary," said Nina. "You put your thoughts in there and stuff?"

"Not really. I make a record of what I see," said Ada.

"Uh-huh," said Nina. "So . . . a little bit like a di—"

"Like a field guide," said Ada. "You know, like what a scientist might keep."

"So, you wouldn't, like, write a poem about Marguerite?" said Nina.

"No. But I try to draw pictures, so I can remember what they look like later," said Ada.

"I love drawing! Is that a rat?" asked Nina.

"That's Marguerite," said Ada.

"Oh yeah. Of course," said Nina.

Nina went home at five. A little while later Ada had dinner with Elliott and her dad. Then she video-chatted with her mom.

"So you met Nina!" said Mom.

"You sent her over, didn't you?" said Ada.

"New friends are good, Ada," said Ms. Lace. "How did you get along?"

"Fine, I guess. Nina is . . . interesting," said Ada. "She's funny . . . quirky. She's not Anna though."

"Nor should she be, Ada," said Ms. Lace. "She's a *new* friend."

"I guess you're right," said Ada.

8:00 p.m. Mom called from Barcelona.
There was a pair of possums by Ms.
Reed's trash can, but they ran away
when she let Marguerite out.

Ada read Charles Darwin's notes on the blue-footed booby until her eyes started to droop. She woke sometime in the night to the sound of Ms. Reed calling out for Marguerite. Ada was too sleepy to get up and look out the window, so she just jotted down a quick note.

12:33 a.m. Ms. Reed just woke me up calling for Marguerite.

Then Ada rolled over and went to sleep again.

Chapter Five
The Disappearing Dog

Ada woke the next morning to Elliott's plastic dagger across her neck.

"Tell me where the booty is, Lady Lace, or I'll slice you open like a sack of molasses!" he sneered.

"Molasses doesn't come in sacks," said Ada with her eyes still closed. "And that dagger wouldn't slice a soft-boiled egg, Elliott Lace."

"That's 'Bluebeard' to you, missy!" said Elliott.

She opened an eye to see Elliott with a blue Magic Marker beard. "Pop! Elliott needs to wash his face!" yelled Ada.

"Ada!" Elliott complained. He bolted out of the room. She heard her father drag Elliott into the bathroom and turn on the water.

"No! That's me blue beard! Nooooooo!"

With the captain out of the way, Ada grabbed her notebook and went to the window.

7:00 a.m. Foggy! Feels like home.

Attendance:

Can just make out a bunch of sparrows and maybe a goldfinch. So quiet. Does fog affect sound? (Investigate this further.)

7:30 a.m. Yes! Fog absorbs high sound frequencies. Interesting . . .

Ada peered hard into the whiteness, but she couldn't make anything else out. She decided to look at the *Beagle* book again.

By lunchtime the scene outside of Ada's window had changed.

12:57 p.m. The fog has cleared!

Nina just waved at me from the back alley.

I wonder how long it will take her to come upstairs.

12:58 p.m. 30 seconds.

"What's new on *Popperly Way*?" asked Nina.

"It's been quiet," said Ada.

Just then they heard another engine outside. Both Ada and Nina rushed to the window—although Ada rushed a little more slowly.

"What could he have this time? A boat?" said Ada, smirking.

"No, it's still the truck. . . . Oh! Ha! That's funny," said Nina.

Milton zoomed his truck around in figure eights through the garden. He tried to chase some squirrels, but they just ran up into the trees. There was no sign of Marguerite or Ms. Reed. After a few minutes Milton got bored and left.

"I guess Ms. Reed got smart about Milton, huh? She must have let Marguerite out earlier," said Nina.

"Actually, I haven't seen them all day," said Ada. "It was really foggy this morning, so I guess they could have been out earlier. But I haven't heard any barking."

"Maybe they went away?" Nina said.

"But I heard Ms. Reed calling Marguerite late last night," said Ada.

"Maybe they were abducted by aliens!" said Nina.

"That's an . . . interesting theory, but . . ."

"No, listen. I know you just moved here," said Nina. "But the Bay Area is a totally magical place. It's got one of those special doors, you know? Like to other realities."

"Okay," said Ada, trying to be polite. "But it will be hard to prove. And there's probably a simpler explanation. That's Occam's razor."

"Oxham's what now?" asked Nina.

"Occam's razor," said Ada. "It says the simplest theory is usually the best. It's easier to test."

"Hmm, great point. So she was probably abducted by aliens, then. That's the simplest solution!" said Nina. Ada almost laughed, but then she realized Nina was serious.

"Well," said Ada, "why don't we see if the dog's really missing first and go from there?"

"Good plan!" said Nina. "You are so smart. I'm glad we're friends!"

• • •

Later that night, the phone rang.

"So, guess what?" It was Nina.

"What?" asked Ada.

"You're not going to guess?" asked Nina.

"You saw the aliens?" Ada guessed. "They bought Ms. Reed and Marguerite an ice cream and then dropped them off at home?"

"I wish! That would be so much cooler!" said Nina. "I saw Ms. Reed on the way home, and she wasn't with Marguerite. Doesn't she always have Marguerite with her? She seemed sad, too."

"Oh no," said Ada. "I hope a coyote didn't get her."

"Don't even say that!" cried Nina.

"Sorry," said Ada. "She'll come back. Maybe she's just . . . on an adventure?"

"Or maybe she was dognapped!" said Nina.

"Dognapped? By aliens?"

"No, seriously!" said Nina. "I was going to say . . . Milton."

"Really?" said Ada. "But why?"

"Just to be mean! You've seen what he does to Marguerite. He's not interested in anyone unless he can mess with them. Maybe he got mad that Ms. Reed kept threatening to tell his mom, so he decided to get even."

"Hmmm . . . interesting . . ."

"Are you being sarcastic?"

"No. You may be onto something. He certainly is a prime suspect. I'll keep an eye out. We'll need to step up our surveillance."

Ada gazed longingly at the gecko gloves on her shelf. The gloves allowed the wearer to scale vertical surfaces . . . just like a gecko! She'd made them last month but hadn't had a chance to try them out. If only she weren't injured, she could use them to climb Milton's building and peek into his window. She looked across the way. There was a big old ginkgo tree just outside his building. It had a long, sturdy branch that extended nearly to Milton's windowsill. The perfect place to set a spy camera.

"Do you like to climb trees, Nina?" Ada asked.

"It's only my favorite pastime!" Nina exclaimed.

Chapter Six

The Snake's Snake

Ada looked through the window all morning. She studied Milton's apartment. Part of her hoped she'd be able to see enough through her binoculars so they wouldn't have to plant a camera. But part of her liked the challenge. She just wished she were the one doing the climbing.

At 3:00 Nina arrived with her sleeping bag and pajamas for a sleepover. A minute later Ada's dad popped in.

"Do you girls want to play a game? Or we could bake some cookies," he said.

Ada knew she couldn't tell him she and Nina were planning to spy on the neighbor. He wouldn't like it, even if the neighbor was a nine-year-old kid who teased dogs.

“Actually, Dad, we’d like to just play together,” said Ada.

“Okay,” said Mr. Lace. He seemed disappointed, but he left anyway.

Ada felt like a fraud. Nina seemed to hear her thoughts.

“Don’t worry, Ada. We just have to rescue Marguerite and catch that beast Milton.”

“He is a bully, but do you really think he stole Marguerite?” said Ada.

“Well, that’s why we’re looking for evidence, right?” said Nina.

Nina had a point. Besides, this was the most fun Ada had had since moving to San Francisco.

They watched Milton’s building until they saw him leave the apartment. When he passed through the alleyway toward Polymer, they sprang into action.

"This is the camera," said Ada. "You need to get on that branch by the window. It has the clearest view of Milton's room. Place it close enough so we can see clearly, but not so close that he'll see it."

"Okay," said Nina.

"And take this walkie-talkie," said Ada. "I've modified it to work over longer distances, and also I installed a panic button on the side in case of emergencies."

"Cool!" said Nina.

Ada had already linked up the wireless camera to her tablet. She watched through the window as Nina made her way across the garden and up to Milton's apartment. Nina looked around to see if the coast was clear. A man passed by on the garden path, looking at his phone. When he was gone, Nina jumped up to grab the lowest branch, pulled herself up, and swung her leg over. Ada was impressed. Maybe Nina was a born spy.

Ada watched the jumpy camera view from her tablet as Nina made her way out on the big branch by Milton's window. Within five minutes Nina had the camera secured to the branch and pointed into the window. A couple of minutes later Nina was back in Ada's room.

"How'd I do?" asked Nina.

"It's perfect! Look, here comes Milton," said Ada.

The girls watched Milton through the window as he crossed the courtyard and entered his apartment building. Then they turned their attention to the tablet.

Milton walked into his bedroom and headed straight to a tank with a big stick in it. There was a fat snake coiled around the stick.

"Wow. He's got a rosy boa in there," said Ada.

Ada didn't know whether to be impressed or disgusted. Snakes were fascinating, but she wasn't sure how she felt about keeping them in a tank.

Milton took the snake out and draped it across his shoulders.

"What kind of a creep has a pet snake?" said Nina.

He petted the snake's head for a while and then set it back in the tank. He walked out of the room and came back in with something in his hand. Ada zoomed in. Milton held his hand up to his eye. He was holding something small and furry. He was nose to nose with it.

"Is that a little mouse?" said Nina. "Awwww . . ."

Ada glanced over at Nina, waiting for her to realize what was going to happen next.

"Oh no!" Nina cried.

Before Ada could stop her, Nina bolted out of her room, down the steps, and across the garden to Milton's apartment. Within a minute Ada saw Nina climb the stairs and pound on Milton's door. The door opened, and Nina disappeared from view and reappeared on the tablet in Milton's room. That girl was fast. Milton looked at her, confused. He looked at the mouse and then out the window. In one fell swoop Nina had compromised their entire operation.

Chapter Seven

Back to the Window

Ada tried to reason with her friend. "The snake has to eat, Nina."

"I know! I know!" said Nina. She was holding the rescued mouse in her hand. "But just look at this little guy! And Milton was enjoying it way too much. Did you see him? Couldn't he just feed it bugs or something? He's not just a dognapper, he's a killer!"

"Did you see a dog in there?" Ada asked.

"No," said Nina.

"Well, then he's just a killer," said Ada.

"Maybe he already fed Marguerite to the snake!" cried Nina.

"I don't think so," said Ada. "That dog may be tiny, but it's way too big for that snake to eat."

Nina sunk onto Ada's bed.

"Do you think Milton will tell?" asked Ada.

"Probably, just for fun," said Nina.

There was a knock at the door.

"There's a boy here," said Mr. Lace. "He says he's a friend of Nina's."

"Friend! Pffft!" said Nina.

Milton burst in.

"Hello, hello, hello, ladies!" He turned to Ada. "Milton P. Edison, Esquire. You're the new girl, I presume."

He paused for a second to look over the room and noticed Ada's cast for the first time.

"What'd you do? Trip over your shoelace?" He laughed at his own joke.

"See!" Nina whispered to Ada. "I told you he was a creep."

Ada did see.

"I've got to get the laundry and check on Elliott," said Ada's father. He eyed Milton suspiciously. "You'll be okay?" he asked Ada.

"Yes, yes, yes! Thanks so much, Mr. Lace," said Milton.

"It's fine, Pop," said Ada. "We'll call if we need anything."

When Mr. Lace was gone, Milton turned to Ada and Nina.

"Well, well, well."

"Do you always say everything three times?" Ada asked.

"No, no, n—" Milton looked thrown off for a second then continued. "You girls have quite an operation here, don't you? Let me guess: That camera in the tree is connected to this tablet. Am I right?"

"What do you want, Edison?" asked Ada. She'd never called anyone by their last name. The kid was really making her skin crawl.

"I want in," said Milton.

"Never!" cried Nina.

"This is a two-person project. Do you have another request?" said Ada.

"C'mon, c'mon, c'mon. I know you didn't rig that camera just to rescue that rodent. So what are you two up to?"

"It's none of your business," Nina replied.

"You had a camera outside my window!" Milton yelled.

"Ada!" Ada's dad called from downstairs. "Everything okay?"

"We're fine, Dad!" Ada called back. "All right.

Just keep your voice down. We're trying to find Marguerite."

"Ms. Reed's silly dog? Hahahaha. That's a good one. No, really."

"Really," said Ada. "The dog's missing. We're trying to find her."

He paused and looked at them.

"Girls, girls, girls. When you're done wasting your time on all this cute lost dog stuff and have some real cases to solve, come find me." He handed Ada a business card. "In the meantime, I hope nothing else trips up your uh . . . investigation." With that, he walked out of the room.

"We better watch Milton," Ada said. "He could get in our way."

"I was thinking the same thing. Who's next on our suspect list?" said Nina.

Ada was a little disappointed. There wasn't anyone else on their list. Ada worried that it probably was a coyote. But she knew she shouldn't tell Nina that.

"Well, it's back to the window, I guess," said Ada. "And surveillance . . . Ah, shoot! We forgot to get the camera."

She looked out the window just in time to see Milton in the tree. That couldn't be good.

Chapter Eight

The Greatest Setbacks

Nina left late Saturday morning after Mr. Lace's famous pancakes, and Ada resumed her post at the window. She saw a flurry of sparrows on the tree just outside her window and wondered if they were fighting or just communicating.

10:00 a.m. Cloudy

20 sparrows, 2 squirrels & Mr. Peebles

Still no Ms. Reed or Marguerite.

Observations:

Jacob and Jeanie drank coffee together in their running clothes and watched the feeders. Mr. Peebles left the apartment and stopped to chat with them. He's still dressed in orange coveralls. I *wonder if he has more than one set.*

10:45 a.m. Jacob had changed into blue pants and an old T-shirt. I think it had a picture of an elephant on it. Jeanie came around from the alley, and they walked toward the water.

Ada turned her binoculars toward Ms. Reed's apartment. Since the dog had gone missing, Ms. Reed had barely been outside in the garden. She now stood staring through the door, one hand holding back a flowered curtain. After a minute the curtain dropped.

Ada looked over at Milton Edison's window. She found him staring right back at her—through binoculars. She couldn't see Milton's face that well, but she guessed he looked smug.

That afternoon Nina called.

"I think I have a new lead," she said. "You know that kid Jack?"

"Yeah, he hangs out with Elliott," Ada said.

"Well?" Nina asked.

"You think Jack took Marguerite?" Ada asked.

"He *really* liked her," said Nina.

"That's true, but he's only six!" said Ada.

"But he could be advanced for his age," said Nina.

In the next room she could hear Elliott and Jack making farting noises.

"Maybe, but we should pursue other ideas,

just in case," said Ada. "Maybe Marguerite ended up at the dog shelter."

After dinner Ada tried to reach Anna without any luck. She worked on her illustrations in the field guide. She was feeling self-conscious about her drawing of Marguerite. She also wanted to make sure she had an accurate representation of the garden. The juniper trees ended up looking like scrambled eggs.

Outside, she noticed a little camera that looked a lot like hers. It was attached to a low tree branch out at the edge of the garden. She noticed it was pointed toward her window. She shifted her binoculars over toward Milton Edison's window. Milton was in his room, holding his tablet. She put the binoculars down and picked up her own tablet. On the screen she saw herself in the window, looking at her tablet.

"Oh, Milton, Milton, Milton . . . ," said Ada.

5:30 p.m.

Milton has stolen my camera and is trying to use it to spy on me. He hasn't figured out that he needs the security codes to connect it to his own tablet.

Jeanie is playing the ukulele on Jacob's stoop.

Mr. Lace and Elliott wandered into the room.

"Wow. The music is nice, isn't it?" said Mr. Lace. They sat together and listened.

"This has shaped up to be a nice little room, hasn't it, Adita?" said Mr. Lace.

"It certainly has, Pop. I didn't think I would be spending quite so much time in it so soon, but the view is nice."

When the song ended, Jacob walked out of the garden through the little alley. Jeanie started a new song.

Elliott got antsy. He spilled a glass of water and nearly soaked Ada's field guide.

"Ell, why don't you take O and H into your room for a little while," Ada suggested.

"I CAN?!" said Elliot.

"Sure, but don't let them run away," said Ada. Ada was glad she had turtles for pets.

"You're a good big sister, Ada," Mr. Lace said.

"I'm going to go start dinner. I'll call you when it's ready."

"Sounds good, Pop."

Jeanie finished her tune, and Jacob returned with a bundle of pink flowers. Jeanie stood up and gave Jacob a hug.

Mr. Peebles walked by with his arms full of two big bags. One was from the Pet Pen, the other was stuffed with what looked like a carpet remnant, foam rubber, and a bunch of wires. He smiled and nodded to Jacob and Jeanie and hurried up the stairs. Ada made a note of it in her field guide.

I wonder if Jacob and Jeanie are dating. And I wonder what Mr. Peebles is feeding his fish.

Chapter Nine

Chance Favors the Prepared Mind

Sunday morning was surprisingly busy in Juniper Garden. Ada woke to the smell of baking. Her stomach growled. She hoisted herself into her chair and saw Jeanie moving around her apartment. There was a little bouquet in her window.

9:00 a.m. Low clouds
Jacob is filling his feeders.
Jeanie looks like she's cooking something.
She's got an apron on.

An hour later Ada saw Jeanie come through the alley and across the garden carrying two baskets.

Jeanie left bundles of goodies at Ms. Reed's door. She seems very kind.

It seemed that Ada and Nina weren't the only ones thinking about Ms. Reed.

Nina came over in the afternoon.

"I stopped by the dog shelter yesterday," said Nina, "just to see if Marguerite ended up there."

"Good idea. Did you find anything?" said Ada.

"There's an adorable little dog that looks almost exactly like Marguerite. I thought I had found her! But it was a boy," said Nina.

"Oh. Oh well," said Ada.

"He was really cute, though!" said Nina. "And there's still *Jack* to consider."

"Nina, Jack's a good kid," said Ada.

"But I know he had his eye on Marguerite! And maybe *because* he's so little, he didn't know any better," said Nina.

"Hmm . . . ," said Ada.

"I think we should look into it," said Nina.

"Well," said Ada, "I guess I'll put him on the list of suspects."

• • •

The next morning Elliott went on a tour of Alcatraz with Jack and his family. Ada helped Elliott tie his parrot on extra tight before he left.

"I'll be back with the booty, or me name isn't Bluebeard," said Elliott.

Ada was a little jealous of Elliott. She had read about the historic escape from Alcatraz. In the 1960s, four prisoners at Alcatraz had planned an escape for months without anyone noticing. Using spoons, they widened the ducts in their cells. They set up a workshop on the roof to build boats and tools. They made decoy dummies of themselves out of soap and toilet paper. No one knew for sure what happened to the men, but many believed they made it to Mexico.

Even though they were criminals, Ada couldn't help but admire them. Their plan had taken cleverness, determination, and discipline.

But Ada also wondered why no one had noticed. The dummies were too poorly painted to look like real men. And the prisoners had stolen prison supplies. Maybe the guards were looking for the wrong things.

Ada suddenly realized that she was not so different from the guards. She had been watching the courtyard for days, and there was one person who had clearly been planning something. One person who was at work on something quite different from the rest of his neighbors. The clues had been there all along, and she had missed them.

Chapter Ten

The Littlest Suspect

Later that afternoon Nina stopped by just as Elliott and Jack were getting back from the harbor. Ada heard her father greet Nina at the door and return to his office. Then she heard Nina talking to Jack.

"Come on, Jack," said Nina. "Just tell me where the pup is."

Ada hobbled downstairs and into the kitchen. Elliott was stuffing a cookie into his mouth. Jack looked like he was about to burst into tears.

"I just played with her sometimes!" cried Jack.

"Nina!" said Ada. "The probability of a six-year-old stealing a dog and getting away with it is very low."

"Well, he's not getting away with it!" said Nina. "I caught him!"

Tears trickled down Jack's cheeks.

"Oh gee . . . ," said Nina. She snapped out of her bad-cop routine. "Maybe you're right, Ada. I'm sorry, Jack."

"Give your friend a cookie, Elliott," said Ada. "Come on, Nina. We have work to do."

Once they got to Ada's room, Ada told Nina the new theory.

"Mr. Peebles has been carrying lots of weird stuff up to his apartment," said Ada.

"He always carries weird stuff up to his apartment," said Nina.

"But big bags from the Pet Pen?" said Ada. "It's way too much stuff for a few fish. There he is!"

Mr. Peebles was carrying a long black box with a handle. It had a zippered opening at the top and one at the side.

"What do you think that is?" Ada asked. She passed the binoculars to Nina.

"My grandma uses one of those to bring her cat to the vet!" said Nina. "Where do you think Mr. Peebles is going to take Marguerite?"

"I don't know. But we better figure it out before Marguerite disappears for good!" said Ada.

Chapter Eleven

Occam's Shaver

The next morning it was quiet in the garden. Hours passed with no activity. And Ada hadn't seen any signs of Mr. Peebles. She looked through her telescope, but that wasn't much better than the binoculars. He had to be on the other side of his apartment.

Nina flurried in just after lunch.

"What's happening?" she asked.

"I don't know. I can't see anything!" said Ada.

"Maybe Mr. Peebles left town with her! He figured out that we're onto him!" said Nina.

"It's possible," said Ada. Hearing Nina be so frantic made Ada feel calmer and more focused. "But we should check to see if he's somewhere else in the apartment first. Or if he's just out for a while."

"He left Marguerite all alone!" said Nina.

"We don't even know if Marguerite is—"

"ALIVE! Oh no, Ada!"

"Let's start with the simplest explanation," said Ada.

"Occam's shaver!" said Nina.

"*Razor*. If she's in there, he probably just borrowed her." Ada paused. "*Borrowed* her? Why would Mr. Peebles 'borrow' a dog? I'm starting to sound as crazy as . . ."

Nina's eyes narrowed.

Ada looked at the floor, then at the corner of her bed, then through her binoculars again.

"As crazy as who, Ada?" Nina asked.

"I didn't mean 'crazy,' exactly," said Ada. "I just meant . . ."

"I'm crazy, huh?" said Nina. Ada was surprised. She had never seen Nina angry before. Ada was not fond of fighting, especially with her only friend in San Francisco.

"If I'm so crazy," Nina said, "I guess you can investigate without me. Good luck climbing trees!"

"Nina . . . ," Ada said.

"This whole thing was your CRAZY idea anyway, remember?" said Nina. She stormed out.

Actually, it was Nina who thought the dog had been kidnapped, but this seemed like the wrong time to mention it.

Chapter Twelve

Ada Goes Solo

Later that afternoon Elliott zipped into Ada's room, sword held high. "LADY ADA!!!" he shouted.

"Yes, Captain," said Ada. "I'm right here—you don't have to yell."

"The bloke across the way has offered me passage on his ship in exchange for giving you this message," said Elliott. He handed Ada an envelope.

Ada glanced through the window. Milton was in the garden, staring straight up at her. Ada opened the envelope. Inside was her camera. It was in pieces. It would take her days to figure out how to put it back together.

"Great," she said.

“Aye!” said Elliott. “He is a scurvy dog, but he has a yar vessel!”

“Don’t trust him, Ell,” she said. But Elliott was gone before he heard.

By five o’clock there was still no sign of Mr. Peebles. Ada was feeling bad about Nina. She was lost without her new friend. Not just because of the case, either. For the past few days she and Nina had worked so well together. Plus, the investigation was much more fun with Nina's wild theories. Ada had barely had time to be homesick or miss her mom.

But Marguerite needed rescuing, so Ada would just have to get a look at the other side of Mr. Peebles's apartment herself. The problem was that Mr. Peebles's apartment was on the second floor. How was she supposed to see inside his windows? She really needed Nina's help. Ada decided she would apologize to Nina. If that didn't work out, she'd just sit near Mr. Peebles's apartment and try to catch a glimpse of him.

Ada stood on her crutches. Surprisingly, she felt strong and stable. Placing her weight on one crutch, Ada reached up to her lowest shelf for her Darwin book. Right next to it were the gecko gloves. She grabbed them. Maybe she could coax Nina into using them to climb Mr. Peebles's building. She put them in a little backpack with her book, the binoculars, and a little camera. It wasn't as good as the one that Milton had broken, but it would have to do.

She walked down to her father's office.

"Hey, Pop," said Ada.

"Hiya, Adita," said Mr. Lace. "What's happening?"

"I'm going to take a little walk to see Nina. We got in an argument earlier."

"Uh-oh," he said. "I'm sorry to hear that. Are you okay to get there by yourself?"

"It's just on the outside of the garden. I'll be careful. It's safety first from now on."

"Okay, but don't be gone long," said her father.

"Daddy?" Ada asked. She wanted to tell her dad about their investigation. Her little white lie had grown. At least before, she'd had a partner to share it with.

"What is it, sweetie?" asked Mr. Lace.

"Never mind. I love you," said Ada.

"I love you, too, Adita."

Chapter Thirteen

Defying Gravity

Ada walked out into the garden. It was strange walking by all the homes she had studied from her window—like visiting a place that you had seen only on TV. She noticed a coffee cup still on Jacob's patio. Ms. Reed's flowers drooped. She felt a stab of sadness for the woman who had lost her best friend.

When she reached Nina's building, she rang the bell for her apartment. There was no answer. After a minute she rang again, but still, no answer. She decided to go back down the block and wait awhile.

Just across the street from Mr. Peebles's building there was a little triangle with benches and flower beds. A couple of people were sitting, looking at their phones.

She found a bench away from the street and took out her book. There was a tree in front of Mr. Peebles's building, but she could still see most of his window. She thought she saw someone moving around inside. She fished her binoculars out for a better look.

Mr. Peebles *was* in there, but she couldn't see what he was doing or what was in the room. She was dying to know what he was up to.

A few minutes later Mr. Peebles came out the front door and walked down Polymer Street. How many times had he exited from this side without Ada knowing? She looked up at his window through the binoculars. His apartment appeared empty. It was now or never. With her gecko gloves, she could climb the front of his building, place the camera, and make her way back down. But could she make it without being seen? Nina had climbed up the tree near Milton's apartment in seconds, but she didn't have a cast on one of her legs. Ada was afraid. But she was also determined.

When she was in front of Mr. Peebles's building, she looked around to make sure no one was watching. Then she sat down on the stoop and pulled out the gecko gloves. She slipped them on and put her gloved hands against the wall—they held firmly. It was exciting! Slowly and cautiously, she began to scale the building. She had always wanted to be able to cling to walls like a lizard. She had to jam her cast against the wall, but she made her way up to Mr. Peebles's window and peered inside.

Ada couldn't believe her eyes! Mr. Peebles had a lab beyond her wildest dreams! There were computers that all seemed to be running different

scenarios
and predicting
outcomes. In the
corner was a set of
shelves with toolboxes labeled in
black Magic Marker: bolts, transistors, resistors, capacitors, rivets . . . all the basic necessities for making cool gadgets. The other side of the room had shelves from floor to the ceiling that were

filled with books. It was better than Disneyland! Ada had to stop herself from climbing inside.

She was just reaching for the little camera when—

"BARK!"

Ada was so startled, she jerked back away from the windowsill. The gecko gloves lost contact with the wall, and she fell with a crash.

"Oh . . . ow!"

The fall had knocked the air out of Ada; she was struggling to breathe. She still had no air in her lungs and was starting to panic. Ada had no idea how long Mr. Peebles would be gone. She had to get out of there before he returned. Then, as if from nowhere, Nina's face appeared above her.

"Ada! Are you okay?" Nina asked.

Ada gasped. She could breathe again!

“Nina! I’m so happy to see you,” said Ada. “I’m really sorry about before. I tried to stop by, but you weren’t there and . . .”

“Never mind,” said Nina. “Let’s get out of here before Peebles catches us!”

Chapter Fourteen

Everything Happens

Nina did her best to walk her bike while also helping Ada.

"You saved me, Nina. Even though I was a jerk," said Ada. "I'm so sorry."

"I know that you weren't being mean," said Nina. "Everyone's a little crazy sometimes, right? It's not such a bad thing."

"What I did sure was crazy," said Ada.

"Did you climb all the way up to his window?" asked Nina.

"Yeah. I would have been fine, but I got startled. By a . . . bark," said Ada.

"So he does have Marguerite!" said Nina.

"Well, I'm not sure. It didn't really sound like Marguerite. In fact, it didn't sound like any dog I've ever heard before."

"Really? Well, what was it?" asked Nina.

"I don't know," said Ada.

They stopped at Nina's building so she could drop off her bike and let her mom know she had to help Ada. Then they continued slowly toward Ada's house.

"It's so lucky that I happened by when I did. It was—"

"A really happy coincidence?" asked Ada.

"Yeah," said Nina. "And, you know, everything happens for a reason."

Ada smiled. Nina was a good friend. They didn't always see things in the same way, but that wasn't a bad thing.

When they got to Ada's door, Ada realized that she had no idea what to tell her father. Nina rang the bell. They heard footsteps inside and then the door opened.

"Girls!" he said. Then he looked at Ada closely.

He pulled a leaf from her hair and examined her cracked cast. "What happened?"

"She tripped," said Nina.

"Oh, Ada," said Mr. Lace. "Let's get you upstairs."

Nina took Ada's backpack and followed them. Mr. Lace got Ada settled and then turned to Nina.

"Do you need to get home, Nina? It's going to be dark soon."

"Can Nina stay for a bit?" asked Ada.

"Okay, but only five minutes," said Mr. Lace.

"You got it, Mr. Lace," said Nina. Ada's father seemed satisfied and left.

"Do you think you can plant this camera in the tree in front of Mr. Peebles's apartment?" Ada asked Nina.

"No sweat," said Nina. "Maybe I can take a peek while I'm up there."

Ada looked out the window just as Mr. Peebles came out of his building.

"Nina, it's Mr. Peebles!" she said.

Mr. Peebles walked to the far end of the street to one of the neighbor's trash cans. He stopped and looked around, as if making sure that no one was watching him. Then he opened up the trash can and slid something from under his coveralls into it. He closed the lid and headed back inside.

"What do you think it was?" asked Nina.

"I don't know, but we have to find out," Ada replied.

"Gotcha," said Nina. "I'll take a look on the way home and let you know."

"Okay. Be careful!" said Ada. "I'll see you tomorrow."

Nina grabbed the little camera and left. Ada watched out the window as Nina slid stealthily along the buildings at the edge of the garden toward the trash can. She looked to the right. She looked to the left. Then she quickly pushed the lid of the trash can off, peeked inside, and popped it back on and headed toward her apartment. A few minutes later Ada heard a chime. She checked her tablet. There was a message from Nina: *Milk-Bones*.

7:20 PM
TEXT MESSAGE
NINA
Milk-Bones.

Chapter Fifteen

The Final Suspect

The next day Mr. Lace took Ada to see the doctor. Ada would have to stay in a cast for a few extra days to be safe. They replaced the old cast, because it had cracked in the fall. Ada's mom was due home later that day, and Ada hoped that she didn't ask too many questions. Ms. Lace *always* asked more questions than Mr. Lace.

When she got home, Ada parked herself by the window. Nina had set up the camera in the tree, as planned. Ada watched the back room on the tablet and kept her eye on the garden windows at the same time.

1:00 p.m. Blue sky, sun, big puffy white clouds

25 or so sparrows, 1 chipmunk, 3 squirrels

Observations:

Mr. Peebles came in and checked some of the monitors, picked up a coil of wire, and left the room.

Ada was beginning to have doubts about invading another neighbor's privacy. Every time she saw Mr. Peebles talking with Jacob, he seemed quite pleasant. Would he really hurt someone's beloved pet? Sure, he brought odd things home, but they didn't seem to be harmful. In fact, some of the things that Ada collected might be considered odd too. She glanced at the soil samples she'd brought from West Virginia.

Just then she saw Mr. Peebles staring out his window down at the garden. Ada looked through her binoculars and saw him putting what looked like a small, furry animal into a garbage bag. Then he left the room. After a few minutes she saw him exit the garden through the alley, carrying the trash bag.

Ada gasped. She raced to the phone and called Nina.

"Come over!" she said.

After what seemed like an eternity, Nina arrived.

"You're finally here!" cried Ada. "I think Mr. Peebles shoved Marguerite in a garbage bag . . . and put her in the trash!"

"Oh no!" cried Nina.

"I don't know, but I think you better stay over tonight."

"Is it okay with your dad?" said Nina.

"It's usually okay with my dad," said Ada, "but my mom gets home in—"

"Ada love!" Ada's mother burst in the room, ran straight to Ada's chair, and hugged her.

Ada's heart rate skyrocketed.

"And you must be Nina! Hello!"

"Welcome home, Ms. Lace!" said Nina.

Ada tried to slip the binoculars under a chair cushion, but she wasn't fast enough.

"What's happening here?" Ada's mom said, eyeing the binoculars, the tablet, and the telescope.

"Uh . . . ," Ada said.

"We're studying the urban ecosystem!" said Nina.

"That's right! I'm telling Nina about field guides, and she's helping me observe Juniper Garden."

"Hmm . . . well, okay," said Ms. Lace.

Ada convinced her mother to let Nina stay

the night. Ada could tell that her mom was happy that Ada had made a friend. Nina rushed home to grab some clothes and a toothbrush. On the way back she ran into Milton. Ada saw them arguing in the garden.

"Get lost, Milton P. Edison," Nina yelled. "You don't know what you're talking about. You never do!" In a minute she was back in Ada's room.

"What happened?" asked Ada.

"Just Milton being Milton. He knows we're watching Mr. Peebles," said Nina.

"We need to find out for sure if Mr. Peebles took Marguerite before Milton gives us away," said Ada.

Ada and Nina kept their eyes glued to the tablet. Mr. Peebles moved back and forth from the lab to the window across from Ada's. Occasionally, he seemed to be talking to someone. Someone at floor level—like a small dog, perhaps.

"If only we could see below the windowsill," said Ada. "Oh, look! He's leaving."

"I could sneak into his apartment!" said Nina.

"How will you get in?" Ada asked.

"Don't worry, I'll find a way," said Nina. Ada had

learned enough about Nina to know this was true.

"Okay, but be careful." Ada handed Nina one of her walkie-talkies. "Press the emergency button if you get into trouble."

Ada watched Nina cross the garden. Then she watched the tablet, waiting for her friend to appear on the screen.

Out of the corner of her eye she saw Milton come out of his building and run around the fence and up the alley.

"What is he up to?" she wondered.

Back on the tablet, Nina was framed in the second floor hallway window right next to Mr. Peebles's apartment. When Ada looked into the garden again, Milton was walking back through the alley with Mr. Peebles!

"Oh, great." Ada picked up her walkie-talkie. "Nina, come in, Nina. Over."

Nina didn't answer.

Ada looked down at the tablet. Nina was

climbing out of the hallway window. Ada held her breath. Nina maneuvered herself over to Mr. Peebles's lab window and pushed it open. Once inside Nina faced the camera and waved. She moved around Mr. Peebles's lab, then dropped out of sight. Suddenly, a fuzzy face appeared on the tablet.

"Ah!" Ada screamed.

It was a squirrel. There was a flurry of leaves, and the camera dropped to the ground.

Ada tried to call Nina again. "Nina! Nina! Come in!"

Ada's mom walked in. "Hi, girls. I have some shortbread—where'd Nina go?"

"Um . . . ," Ada answered.

Ada turned to the window. Milton Edison was back in his apartment staring straight at Ada's window. She turned to Mr. Peebles's window—he was inside feeding the fish.

Chapter Sixteen

The Marguerite Test

"Oh no!" said Ada.

"Ada? What is it?" said Ms. Lace.

"Uh . . . Nina isn't back," said Ada. "And I'm worried."

Across the street Mr. Peebles walked out of the room with the fish tank. Ada imagined him finding Nina hiding in his lab. Ada looked urgently at her walkie-talkie, as if she could will a warning over it.

"Ada Lace," said Ms. Lace. "Spill it. Now."

"Oh, Mommy. I don't know what I've done!" said Ada. "Nina is hiding in Mr. Peebles's apartment!"

"What?" said Ms. Lace. "Why?"

"Well," said Ada, wondering where to begin.

"You can explain later," said Ms. Lace. "We better go get Nina before she's in real trouble."

Ada's mom and Ada made their way to Mr. Peebles's.

Ada could see Milton in his window, smirking at her.

Ms. Lace rang the bell, and after a long minute Mr. Peebles answered the buzzer and let them up. It was strange to see him up close. He

had a pleasant, round face. He definitely didn't look like a dog killer.

"Oh, hello! You must be Nina's friend!" Mr. Peebles said to Ada. "And you are Ms. Lace?"

"Yes," said Ada's mother. "How are you, Mr. Peebles?"

"Good, thanks. Come in," said Mr. Peebles. "I'm sure you're very curious about what your friend has been up to."

Ada and her mother followed Mr. Peebles into his apartment.

They were greeted by Marguerite. She wiggled all over. Mr. Peebles bent to scratch her ears. Ada was relieved to see the dog was happy.

"I'm so sorry about this. I don't know what the girls were thinking," said Ms. Lace.

"Oh no, please," said Mr. Peebles. "They were curious. There should be more curious people in the world."

Mr. Peebles opened the door to his lab. "I've been working on building the perfect pet—which Marguerite certainly is. I only planned to keep her a day or so, take some videos and give her back before Ms. Reed missed her too much."

Ada heard a familiar, awkward mechanical barking.

"BARK! BARK!"

They followed Mr. Peebles into the lab. It was even more spectacular than Ada remembered.

"Wow," Ada said.

On top of the computers and shelves and shelves of books and manuals of all different kinds, there were three drones piled by the window. Unlike Milton's toy drone, these had been custom built. Stacked on shelves in the corner were several half-finished dog robots. Nina was in the corner playing with one of the models.

"Sit, Rodney!" Nina said to the robo-dog.

BOLTS
TRANSISTORS

The dog sat. It had long silky fur and big brown eyes like Marguerite, but the eyes shifted around unnaturally. Then there was his bark.

"BARK! BARK!" said the robot dog.

"Good dog!" said Nina. "Isn't he sweet?"

"Well . . . ," said Ms. Lace. "He's certainly an accomplishment, Mr. Peebles."

"I'm glad you think so. But he's missing something, and quite a bit of it. I tried to use Marguerite as a model, but Rodney's not the companion she is. I just can't get the coding right," said Mr. Peebles.

"RRRRRUCK!" said Marguerite.

"BARK!" said Rodney. Ada could see immediately what Mr. Peebles meant. Rodney was doglike, but his movements were awkward and mechanical. She wondered if you could give the Turing test to a dog. In the Turing test a person talks to a computer. If the computer can trick the person into believing it is also human, that means the computer passes the test.

It was clear that Rodney hadn't passed the Marguerite test. Marguerite was never going to sniff that robot's butt.

"I don't see how I can ever get Rodney to be as lovely as Marguerite," said Mr. Peebles.

"But you still have to give her back," said Ada.

"Oh, I know," said Mr. Peebles. The buzzer rang. "That will be Ms. Reed."

"Oh," said Ms. Lace. "So you really just . . . borrowed her."

"As I said," said Mr. Peebles. He pressed the door lock button.

Rodney made what Ada guessed was a whining noise, but it sounded more like a rusty hinge. Then he waddled over to the door and dropped a pile of batteries on the carpet.

"Bad boy, Rodney!" said Nina.

"It's okay, Nina," said Mr. Peebles. "He'll never be a real dog." He opened the door for Ms. Reed.

"Oh, hello, girls, Ms. Lace," said Ms. Reed. "May I *please* have my Marguerite back now, Mr. Peebles? I'm lost without her."

Marguerite yelped and squealed. She made happy figure eights around her mistress's ankles.

"There's a good girl," said Ms. Reed.

"She's all yours. Thank you,

Edna," said Mr. Peebles. "She has been a delight!"

"You don't have to tell me!" said Ms. Reed. "I'm off to finish my needlepoint. Ta!"

"Well, there goes another failed project," said Mr. Peebles.

"You just need more time," said Ada.

"But I've lost my model," said Mr. Peebles.

"I think I know where you can find a good replacement," said Nina. "He might not be exactly the same as Marguerite, but at least you get to keep him."

Chapter Seventeen

Back to School

The first day of school had seemed so far away at the start of the summer, but suddenly it was upon them. Ada was excited but nervous. She'd never been the new girl before. Luckily, she had a friend already. She also had a boot to replace her cast, which allowed her to move around better.

The day after the girls had found Marguerite, they had accompanied Mr. Peebles to the dog shelter. Mr. Peebles was thrilled with his new companion, Alan. Nina was right. The dog looked a lot like Marguerite. And he seemed to love Mr. Peebles right away. Marguerite and Alan became fast friends. Sometimes they let Rodney tag along too.

Nina and Ada walked to school with Mr. Lace and Captain Bluebeard—only he was Elliott the Magnificent now. He wore a cape and a hat and carried a wand.

"Behold! A perfectly normal top hat," said Elliott. He reached into the hat. "But inside . . . a little turtle."

"Elliott!" said Ada. "You can't bring Hydrogen to school!"

"But she's my assistant," said Elliott.

"She can assist you when you get home," said Mr. Lace. It was his first day of school too—he was the new art teacher.

Along the way to school they passed Mr. Peebles walking Alan. "See you this afternoon, kids!" Mr. Peebles called.

"He's so nice," Ada said to Nina. "I can't believe we thought he kidnapped Marguerite. And I can't believe he wasn't mad that you snuck into his apartment."

"Well . . . I didn't really sneak in," Nina said.

"But I saw you climb through the window," said Ada.

"I know," said Nina. Her eyes drifted down to the pavement. "I got into the building because Mr. Peebles's neighbor left the door open. But Mr. Peebles came back upstairs just as I was about

to try his door. He invited me in to meet Rodney. So I asked him if I could try climbing through the window. I wanted you to be impressed."

"I am impressed, Nina," said Ada. "I'm impressed by how silly you are!"

Nina gave Ada a gentle punch on the arm.

"It's too bad Mr. Peebles isn't really building a spaceship," said Nina. "Maybe we should build one!"

"I like the way you think, Nina."

Drones

Drones are flying vehicles that you can operate with a remote control. The way a drone flies is similar to a helicopter. A helicopter has propellers, which act like spinning wings. When a propeller spins fast enough, it pushes air down below the helicopter, causing the helicopter to lift up in the air. There are usually four sets of propellers on a drone, which could also be called a "quadcopter" ("quad" meaning "four"). Each propeller helps to lift the drone off the ground! I have friends who connect cameras to their drones and fly them to beautiful areas of San Francisco. That way they can get a drone's-eye view of the city—as long as you have the proper certifications to fly it!

Ecosystem

An ecosystem is a complex community of living things, like plants and animals, interacting together in their environment. I live in San Francisco, so I get to see many of the same ecosystems that Ada does. Ada's urban ecosystem includes her neighbors, their pets, and all of the plants in her backyard. In an ecosystem everyone has their own role to play and contributes something. The actors in an ecosystem often depend on one another in some way.

If you took one neighbor away from Juniper Garden, for example, Ada's ecosystem would be disrupted!

WIRELESS CAMERA

Some wireless cameras can connect to an app on a phone or tablet using Wi-Fi. Once you use your app to connect to the camera, you can see real-time camera footage from your phone or tablet. Because you don't have to be near the camera to be able to see the footage, you can place it up to five hundred feet away and still be able to connect to it remotely. (This makes it a great spying tool for Ada.) I've used wireless cameras to film exciting things that would be too difficult to capture with a handheld camera. I've connected wireless cameras to roller coasters, human centrifuges designed for astronauts (they spin around really fast like a merry-go-round and make an astronaut experience higher gravitational force), and I've even used them underwater to watch astronauts train in a huge pool at NASA!

GECKO GLOVES

The design of gecko gloves is inspired by the gecko's feet. Geckos can stick to surfaces and climb vertical walls because their toes are covered in hundreds of tiny hairs.

The little hairs are so small that they can fit into the contours of walls. An engineering student named Elliot Hawkes at Stanford University used similar principles to create a material that allowed him to climb up walls like Spider-Man! Elliot could be seen scaling walls around campus when he was testing out his gecko gloves design. Each glove has a number of individual reptile-inspired patches with hairlike nanofibers that can cling to surfaces. But remember, not everyone is a gecko! Do not scale walls without the proper equipment and supervision.

Turing Test

The Turing test was developed by a man named Alan Turing to determine if a machine can think like a human. If a computer passes the Turing test, it is considered to be "artificially intelligent" and indistinguishable from a real person. In the test, an evaluator would chat online with two partners: One would be a human and one would be a computer program. If the evaluator couldn't tell which one was the human and which one was the computer, then the computer would pass the Turing test. While some have come close, no computer to date has passed the Turing test. What do you think technology will look like once computers and robots become as smart as humans?

ACKNOWLEDGMENTS

When I was a child I didn't consider myself one of the "smart kids." I dreamed of being a whiz kid like Ada, but instead I was often quiet and unsure of myself. Over time, my wonderful parents helped convince me that with enough hard work, I could accomplish big things and work my way up to become an Ada. I want to thank both of you from the bottom of my heart for your unconditional love and encouragement, especially during my awkward stage. Puberty wasn't kind to me, but you guys made me feel like a pretty rad kid anyway.

Dad, thanks for teaching me how to learn. Mom, thank you for showing me how to love and care for others. Now, and always, you two are my heroes.

To my husband, Tommy, whom I fell in love with at a NASA internship after you taught me how to solve a Rubik's Cube—thank you for being the feminist partner every girl should have. You make living, loving, exploring, and learning about the universe an endless adventure. I value your advice and opinion on everything I do. Every Ada needs a partner like you to help tackle this magical world.

These books would not have been possible without the incredible guidance and work from Jennifer Keene; my manager, Kyell Thomas; Christian Trimmer; and Liz Kossnar—and everyone else at Octagon and Simon & Schuster. And a very special thank-you to Tamson Weston and Renee Kurilla for giving Ada the words and illustrations to tell my story. I'm so grateful that you all chose to work with me; you have changed my life for the better. Thank you for bringing Ada to life—I wish I had someone like her to look up to when I was younger.

And finally, to all the teachers and professors who go the extra mile, including my little brother Drew—your work is so vitally important and too often underappreciated. Now more than ever, our world needs scientifically literate students who are excited to understand how the universe works. You're making it happen and we can never thank you enough.